*For Talia and Grace Giordano*
*and in loving memory of my parents, Claude and Katharine Broach, who first told me the Story*
—*M.M.*

*For Ben*
—*J.C.*

THIS IS A BORZOI BOOK PUBLISHED BY ALFRED A. KNOPF

Text copyright © 2007 by Marni McGee
Illustrations copyright © 2007 by Jason Cockcroft
All rights reserved.
Published in the United States by Alfred A. Knopf, an imprint of Random House Children's Books, a division of Random House, Inc., New York.
KNOPF, BORZOI BOOKS, and the colophon are registered trademarks of Random House, Inc.
www.randomhouse.com/kids
Educators and librarians, for a variety of teaching tools, visit us at www.randomhouse.com/teachers

McGee, Marni.
A song in Bethlehem / by Marni McGee ; illustrated by Jason Cockcroft. — 1st ed.
p.   cm.
SUMMARY: Wishing to see the kings who are visiting her town of Bethlehem, a beggar girl goes to a stable where she meets, instead,
a young family that gives her a special gift and blessing.
ISBN 978-0-375-83447-9 (trade) — ISBN 978-0-375-93447-6 (lib. bdg.)
1. Jesus Christ—Nativity—Juvenile fiction. 2. Mary, Blessed Virgin, Saint—Juvenile fiction. 3. Joseph, Saint—Juvenile fiction.
[1. Jesus Christ—Nativity—Fiction. 2. Mary, Blessed Virgin, Saint—Fiction. 3. Joseph, Saint—Fiction. 4. Beggars—Fiction.]
I. Cockcroft, Jason, ill. II. Title.
PZ7.M478463Son 2007
[Fic]—dc22
2006035564

The illustrations in this book were created using acrylic paints on watercolor paper.

MANUFACTURED IN MALAYSIA
September 2007

10 9 8 7 6 5 4 3 2 1
First Edition

# A Song in Bethlehem

by Marni McGee

illustrated by Jason Cockcroft

Alfred A. Knopf
NEW YORK

"Three men," whispered Marta the Beggar. "As rich as kings, they were—in their turbans and fur-lined robes. Gold was on their fingers. Rubies hung 'round their necks. Yet I saw them, with my own eyes, in a stable."

Naomi shivered in the chill night air. "I want to see them too," she said.

"Go, then, little one," said Marta, pointing, "to the inn above the crossroads."

Naomi forgot her hunger and ran all the way.
Slipping past travelers, she dashed for the stable door
and peered inside. There were horses, cows, a donkey,
and two brown hens brooding on their nests. A woman
lay in the corner, asleep.

"I came here for nothing," Naomi muttered.
"The kings have gone, if kings they truly were."
Then she saw two boxes, studded with jewels,
nesting in the straw. Beside them was a wooden flute
and a mound of yellow-gold coins.

Quick as a lizard, Naomi dashed inside and snatched one shining coin. As she ran from the stable, a strong hand grabbed her arm.

"Thief!" a voice accused.

Naomi tried to tug free, and the coin fell into the dust. The man drew her into the clearing, where a low fire flickered. Naomi saw his face. His mouth was hidden in bristles of beard. His brows shot out like wings.

"Why, you're no more than a child!" he exclaimed, and his scowl disappeared.

The grumble-voice grew soft. "You're hungry, aren't you?"

Naomi nodded.

The man picked up the coin, then took a bowl and dished thick soup from a pot kept warm beside the fire. He gave it to her along with a chunk of bread.

Naomi ate, thinking of no one and nothing except the food in her mouth and the warmth in her belly. But when she had finished, she remembered where she was and what she had done. She crouched, ready to run.

The man rose. "Don't be afraid," he said, smiling down
at her. "Come. There's someone I want you to see."
The hens rustled their feathers, and the donkey bobbed
its head.

The woman, awake now, sat gazing into a manger. There lay a baby resting on a bed of hay. Light shone from his face as if he were a piece broken from the moon.

Naomi caught her breath.

Crept closer.

Knelt down.

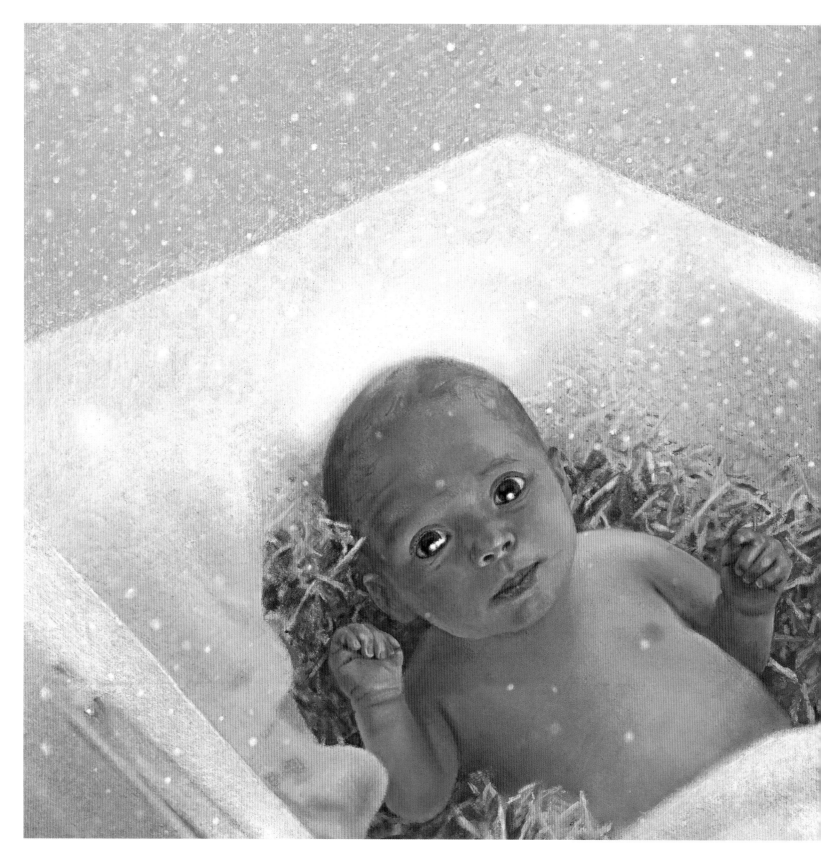

The baby's dark eyes sparkled, and his skin was like hers: the color of rich honey. The air smelled suddenly sweet—as if white lilies had blossomed in the straw.

Naomi felt a sudden bright inside, and her sadness washed away like tangled twigs in a flood-time stream.

The baby's hand reached out. Closed
around her finger.
"Now you have caught me too," she said,
and kissed the baby's brow.

The man looked on, chuckling softly. The woman touched Naomi's sleeve. "Will you stay beside him while I gather our things? We must leave before dawn."

As Naomi bent over the manger, a lullaby came to her lips—a song from a time she no longer remembered.

When the woman was ready, the man helped her
onto the donkey's back and put the baby in her arms.
"Walk with us a ways," he said to Naomi. And
Naomi did.

At the crossroads below the inn, the man said, "I have a gift for you."

Naomi blushed. "I cannot take it, sir. Don't you remember? I stole—"

The man erased her words with his hands. "But the baby caught you. He has claimed you, child, and the gift is *his* to give."

The man reached into his bulging sack and pulled out the wooden flute. "The youngest shepherd—just a boy—gave his flute to the newborn child, and now it shall be yours."

"I don't know how to play it," Naomi protested.

"You will learn," the woman said, "and soon, for blessing lives within its wood."

Naomi could not speak, not even to say goodbye.

She sat on a smooth, flat rock. As the strangers walked away, she lifted the flute and blew.

A single note came out—clean and clear and sweet.

The man turned back and waved.

Naomi laughed aloud, then blew again. Her fingers fumbled at first, but soon they were moving quickly. It was as if she had made this music forever— as if she had always known how.

Music spilled into the valley. It echoed the song that angels sang to shepherds keeping watch on the night the child was born.

As the beggar-girl played, travelers stopped to
listen. Many dropped coins in the grass at her feet.
But Naomi hardly noticed. Her eyes saw only the
flute. Her ears heard only music.

As the morning sun rose above the treetops, Naomi gathered her coins and wrapped them in her scarf.

She ran to the village, where Marta was waiting.

Naomi poured the coins into the old woman's lap. "The night was full of wonders," she whispered. "In the stable was a baby, like no other. He gave me a gift, and somehow I know—we shall never be hungry again."

"I cannot explain . . . and yet I know: my hands have touched a holy child. My lips have kissed a newborn king."